Wednesday Is Spaghetti Day

Do you ever wonder
what your pet cats do when
you leave them home alone?

Written & Illustrated by
Maryann Cocca-Leffler

SCHOLASTIC INC. / New York

Copyright © 1990 by Maryann Cocca-Leffler.

Library of Congress Cataloging-in-Publication Data

Cocca-Leffler, Maryann.
Wednesday is spaghetti day/Maryann Cocca-Leffler.
      p.   cm.
Summary: After her unsuspecting owners leave for work and school, Catrina invites the neighborhood cats over for a festive Italian meal.

ISBN 0-590-42894-2

[1. Cats—Fiction. 2. Cookery, Italian—Fiction.] I. Title.
PZ7.C638We   1990
[E]—dc19   89-6250 CIP AC

12   11   10   9   8   7   6   5   4   3   2   1   0   1   2   3   4   5/9

Printed in the U.S.A.

First Scholastic printing, March 1990   36

To my wonderful parents,
whose Spaghetti Day is
every Tuesday and Thursday!

Love and thanks to
my husband for his support.

It was Wednesday, and for the Tremonte family it was just another day. But for their cat, Catrina, it was not a regular day at all.

Catrina paced impatiently while everyone ate breakfast.

No one could be late today. For today
was Wednesday, and Wednesday is
Spaghetti Day. And all of Catrina's cat
friends were coming for lunch.

Poor kitty,
home all alone
again.

Finally!

As Catrina cleaned up after breakfast, her friends began to arrive. "The kids will be home at three o'clock," she warned. So the cats got right to work preparing lunch.

As Scruffy made the salad and Ruby set the table, Freckles dashed in slamming the door behind him.

"Sorry I'm late," Freckles said. "The kids made me play house with them again."

Freckles quickly took off his bonnet and booties and got to work.

The cats continued cooking . . .

. . . and soon their long awaited Italian lunch was ready.

They sang ... and danced ...

... and toasted each other.

It was wonderful!
None of the cats could remember having
such a feast. But just as they were about
to eat their spumoni ice cream, the clock
struck three. And a school bus pulled up
to the corner!

Ding

Ding

Ding

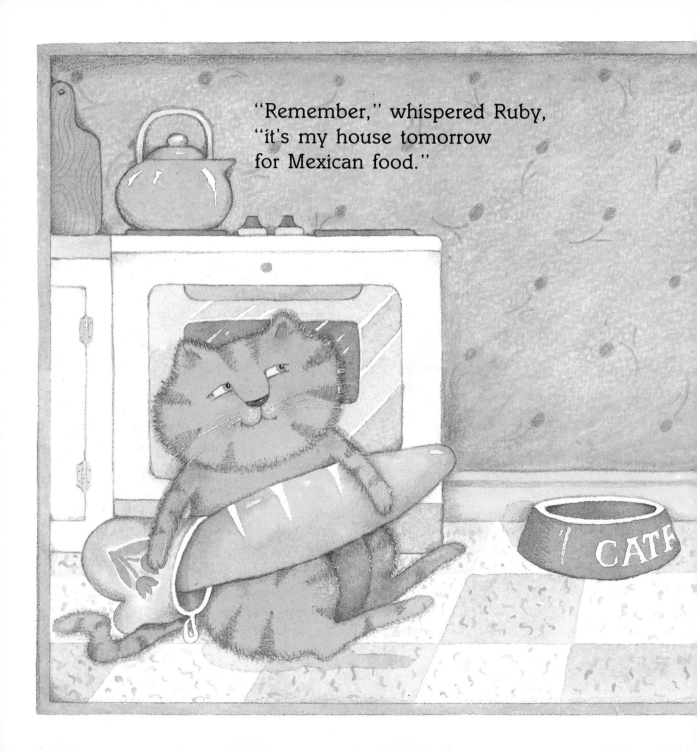

"Remember," whispered Ruby,
"it's my house tomorrow
for Mexican food."

When the kids returned, it was just like any other day.

Here kitty, kitty, kitty!

Catrina walked away fluffing her tail. "No cat food for me," she thought, "tomorrow is another day!"

For tomorrow is Thursday . . .

. . . And Thursday is Guacamole Day!